By Ivy S. Ip
Illustrated by Duendes del Sur

visit us at www.abdopublishing.com

Reinforced library bound edition published in 2013 by Spotlight, a division of the ABDO Group, PO Box 398166, Minneapolis, MN 55439. Spotlight produces high-quality reinforced library bound editions for schools and libraries. Published by agreement with Warner Bros.-A Time Warner Company.

Printed in the United States of America, North Mankato, Minnesota.
102012
012013
This book contains at least 10% recycled materials.

Copyright © 2012 Hanna-Barbera.
SCOOBY-DOO and all related characters and elements are trademarks of and © Hanna-Barbera.
WB Shield: ™ & © Warner Bros. Entertainment Inc.
(s12)

Cover designed by Madalina Stefan and Mary Hall
Interiors designed by Mary Hall

Library of Congress Cataloging-in-Publication Data
This book was previously cataloged with the following information:

Ip, Ivy S.
Clues at the carnival / by Ivy S. Ip ; illustrated by Duendes del Sur.
p. cm. -- (Scooby-Doo! Picture Clue Books)
Scooby-Doo and his friends go to a carnival and investigate the case of the magician's missing hat. Includes rebus clues.
[1. Carnivals--Fiction. 2. Scooby-Doo (Fictitious character)--Fiction. 3. Dogs--Fiction. 4. Rebuses. 5. Mystery and detective stories.]
PZ7.I599 Cl 2001
[E]

2001276643

ISBN 978-1-61479-036-5 (reinforced library bound edition)

, and

were at the carnival.

They wanted to see the and

his in the magic show.

and the gang went to the

magic show .

"There is no magic show today,"
the 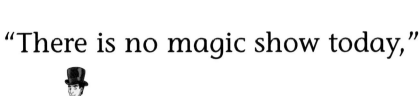 said.

"My magic 🎩 is missing!"
The 🎩 pointed to some 🐾.
"A 🦍 took my 🎩 !" the 🎩
said.

"A 🦍 ?" said 🧑.

"Ruh-roh!" said 🐕.

"We will find your ," said
. ", , and I will
follow the . and will
look for clues."

"But," said, "we might run
into the ."

"Rikes!" said .
 and  were afraid.

"Look, Scoob," said . " !"

 and followed a trail of

 to a booth.

They found a man selling ,

, and .

The was not in the .

The was not near the or

next to the .

 and walked away from

the booth.

 spotted a trail of .

 and followed the .

They found a man selling .

 and looked in between

the .

But the was not there.

, , and  followed

the to a game booth.

Maybe the was inside the

booth.

 looked inside a . He saw

a .

 checked under some .

 looked above the .

But they did not find the or

the .

and  looked for the

on the 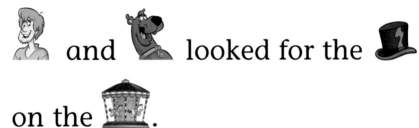.

They met   and .

 saw a and pushed it.

 went around and around

on the !

"Hang on, !"  shouted.

The 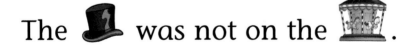 was not on the .

"Jeepers!" 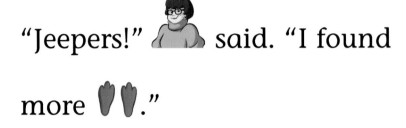 said. "I found

more 👣."

The gang followed the 👣 to

a ⛺.

"What if the 👣 belong to a

🦍?" asked 🧑.

"🐕, will you follow the 👣 for

two 🍿? 🧑 asked.

"Rokay!" 🐕 barked.

🐕 ran inside the ⛺.

A  was juggling some 🔴⚪ inside the ⛺

A 🐰 sat on the 🤡's shoulder.

The 🎩 was on the 🤡's head!

"Jinkies!" 👧 shouted. "The 🤡 has the 🎩!"

The 🤡 was surprised. The 🤡 dropped the 🔴⚪ on his 👢.

The jumped off the .

The hopped over to .

"That made the we

saw!" said.

The ran inside the .

"There is my !" the

shouted. "And there is my !"

"I found the 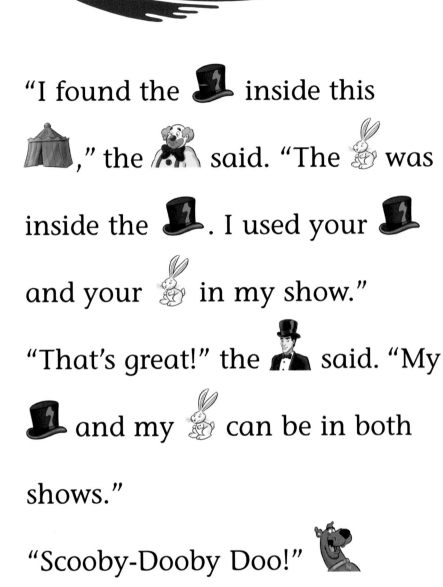 inside this ," the said. "The was

inside the . I used your

and your in my show."

"That's great!" the said. "My

and my can be in both

shows."

"Scooby-Dooby Doo!"

barked.

Did you spot all the picture clues
in this Scooby-Doo mystery?

Reading is fun with Scooby-Doo!